For Robbie, but also for everybody
who has supported and believed in
me along the way.
You know who you are! xox

Published by Britt Harcus
First edition

ISBN 978-0-9954748-0-2 (Paperback)

www.brittharcus.com

JANICE and the SPECIAL BREAKFAST

By Britt Harcus

Janice's eyes ping open. It's 7 o'clock, time to get up.

Time to comb her fleece,
wash her face and
find her boots.

Janice's mammy makes
her a cup of milky tea.
Janice looks for her
little lucky bag.
She's almost ready...

...READY FOR A BIG ADVENTURE!
Janice has been invited across the sea to
eat a special breakfast at Top Chef's House.

JANICE

Please come to mine.
I'll be cooking something fine
Waiting at the waters edge
with my trike + some treats
10 O'CLOCK - DON'T BE LATE
BIG LOVE ♥ T.C X

But Janice is already late.

She kisses her mammy cheerio and runs as fast as her feet will take her.

'Fast feet, fast feet, fast feet!'

'Rush, rush rush!'

Down the steps of the pier she finds Sea Dog waiting.

He's *grumpy*.

As *usual*.

And she forgot her bag.

rover

Meanwhile Top Chef is busy making things in his kitchen...

...*What* a lot of work!

It's a bumpy boat journey out.

Passing the skerries is Janice's *least* favourite bit but the thought of a feast keeps her focused.

There are strange creatures on the skerries. Otters,
eels and seals ahoy! Some are waving. Some are *not*.
Janice shivers. Nearly there...

Suddenly, the boat breaks down!

Janice is handed an oar and together they begin to row ashore.
Not far now! If Janice was *hot* before she is BOILING now.
Her woolly fleece feels scratchy.

And Sea Dog is *still* grumpy.
Those seals, eels and otters don't
seem so far away now. 'EEK!
Keep rowing,' she squeaks.

'WOO HOO! Breakfast is waiting,' bellows Top Chef as they finally arrive.

Janice has *never* been so pleased to see her friend.

She's also VERY hungry.

Sea Dog ties up the boat.
Then he flicks his glasses down
onto his nose and opens his damp
newspaper.

'It's like a different world on this island!' Janice yells.

Top Chef can't hear.

He's in front, pedalling as *hard* as he can. Top Chef lives in a castle on the top of the hill. The tiny trailer bumps up the windy road.

'I hope you're hungry,' Top Chef shouts. 'I've made extra because—'

...Then his voice gets lost in the wind.

'Pick your seat Janice, the rest of the guests are on their way.'

'The *rest*?' Janice eyes up the table. 'How many are coming?' she calls down the hallway.

No reply...

And, just then, the door *bursts* open.
Five seals, two otters and two
eels file in to the room.
They're chattering and
laughing and take *no* notice
of Janice.

Janice has taken note of *them*! These were the scary creatures from the skerry. She feels nervous. Her heart is beating fast.

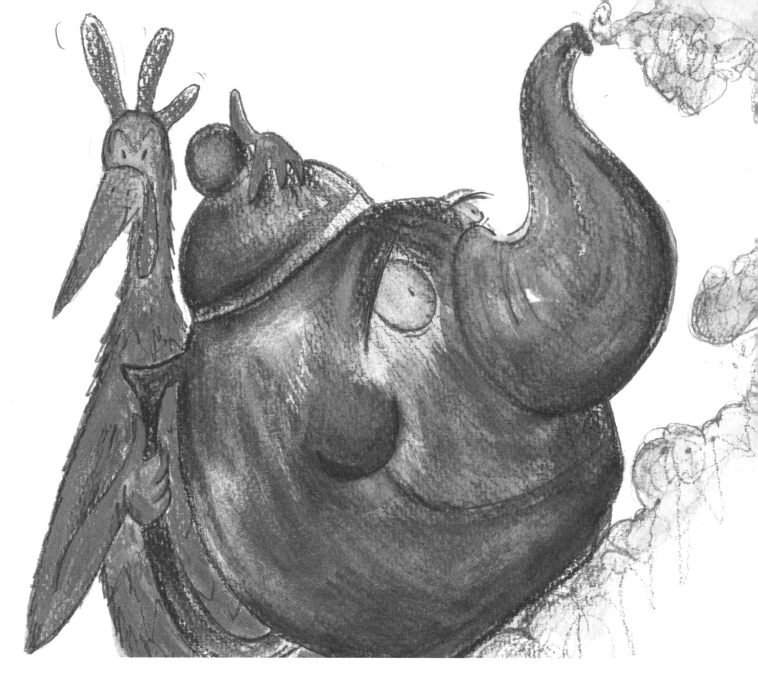

Everyone finds a seat and Top Chef returns holding an enormous teapot. 'Tea with milk?' he asks cheerily. 'Janice, meet my friends from the skerry. Everyone, say hello to Janice!'

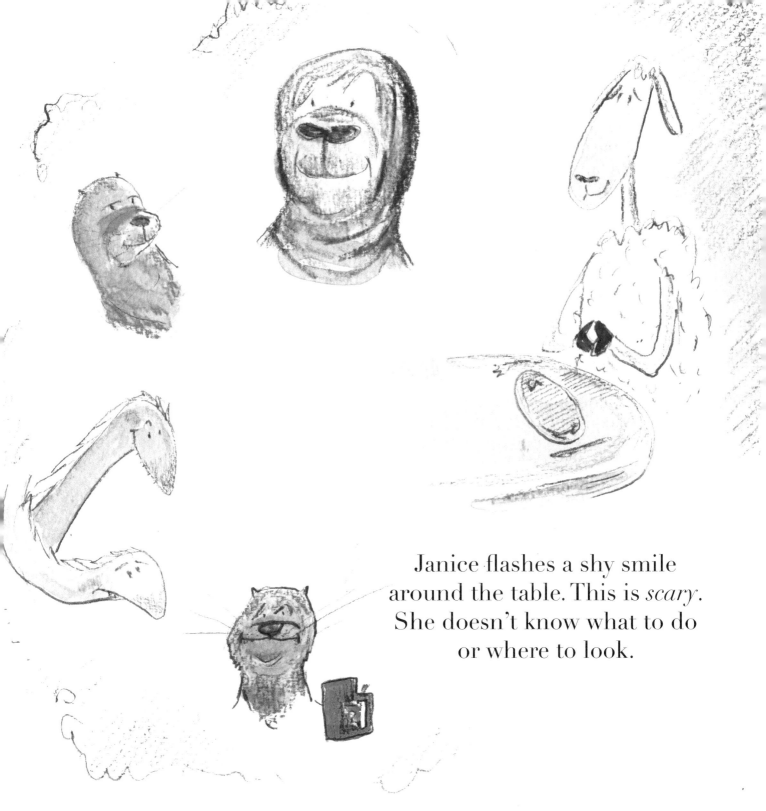

Janice flashes a shy smile around the table. This is *scary*. She doesn't know what to do or where to look.

But the strange creatures flash smiles back. The two small otters
slide onto the seat next to her. One is offering the rhubarb jam.
The other is offering the sticky spoon.
'Oh, em, yes please. Thank you!' stutters Janice.

Slowly she begins to relax and takes a big bite of the hot pancakes Top Chef has prepared. YUM! They taste so delicious.

With clinking cutlery and chomping
mouths it doesn't take long for all
the food to disappear. Then one of
the friendly seals breaks into song.
The eels sway along.
It is *such* fun.

Janice feels warm inside and out. She can't *wait* to tell her mammy when she gets back. Whatever was she even scared of?

'To new friends!' cheers Top Chef.
'NEW FRIENDS!' everybody shouts, before pouring more tea.

At last, it's time to go. Janice says, 'Thank you!' to Top Chef for a brilliant breakfast and a cheery, 'Cheerio!' to all her new friends.

Back to the boat. It's past 1 o'clock already. She's late *again*. But Sea Dog is fast asleep and the boat is still broken. Poor Janice starts to panic a little...

'New friends to the rescue!' exclaims Top Chef, appearing behind her. With that, the seals, otters and eels begin to *push* and *pull* the boat out to sea.

'And we're off!' cheers Janice. She waves happily to everyone.
Top Chef is waving his spotted hankerchief.

Soon enough, Top Chef, the skerry creatures and the big castle are all just a tiny smudge on the horizon. Sea Dog ties up the boat where Janice's mammy is waiting for her.
Janice has *so* much to tell her!
The special breakfast was very special indeed.
Janice will not forget it for a very long time.

And her lost bag?  Sitting *just* where she left it! She didn't need it after all, just the help of her new friends.

THE END

MADE-UP MUCK?

A tall tale or a small tale about life on an Orkney farm

Words and pictures by **Britt Harcus**

Other books by Britt Harcus, including
further Janice adventures, can be found at:

www.brittharcus.com

You can also follow Britt Harcus on

 facebook.com/brittharcus

Twitter@brittharcus

Orkney, Scotland, UK
Thank you

ABOUT BRITT HARCUS

Britt is a farmer's daughter from the beautiful
island of Orkney, just off the North coast of
Scotland. She has been a freelance illustrator
for the past 12 years after studying in Dublin
& Finland.

Britt has an impressive, varied portfolio in
both the private and commercial sector.
This is her third children's book. When not at
work Britt enjoys horse riding and
tea drinking.

Lightning Source UK Ltd.
Milton Keynes UK
UKHW051006081021
391854UK00002B/99